To the little foxes
born in a den
at the edge of a cornfield
just outside town.

1 2 3 4 5 6 7 8 9 10
Library of Congress Cataloging in Publication Data.   Arnosky, Jim. Watching foxes. Summary: While their mother is away from the den, four little foxes play in the sunlight.   1. Red fox—Juvenile literature.   [1. Foxes] I. Title.
QL737.C22A76 1985 599.74'442 84-20157 ISBN 0-688-04259-7 ISBN 0-688-04260-0 (lib. bdg.)
Typography by Kathleen Westray

WATCHING
FOXES

by Jim Arnosky

LOTHROP, LEE & SHEPARD BOOKS
New York

Mother fox leaves
the den to go
hunting.

After the mother
has left, her pups
wake up.

Four little foxes

run outside.

Two pups watch
a bee buzzing by.

Another scratches
a pesky flea.

This little fox
finds a tasty twig
to chew on.

The other pups
want the twig.

One pup pounces
on the other
three.

They all tumble
and growl in a fuzzy
foxy ball.

An ear gets nipped.

A tail gets bit.

Mother
comes home.

The pups greet her

with happy barks.

Mother fox nurses her babies in the warm sunlight.